THE STORY OF
Henry Wadsworth
LONGFELLOW

BY CATHERINE OWENS PEARE

Originally published in 1953

Cover illustration by Nada Serafimovic
Cover design by Phillip Colhouer
Inside illustrations by Margaret Ayer
Originally titled *Henry Wadsworth Longfellow: His Life*

CHAPTERS

Margaret Ayer.

CHAPTER 1
DELIGHT IN THE WOODS AND SEA

I T WASN'T far from here," said Grandfather Wadsworth, waving his hand toward the stretch of woodland, "where Captain John Lovell and his men met up with the Indians."

"Did any of them escape?" asked Henry, who sat at his feet.

"A few," put in Henry's brother Stephen, who knew the story by heart.

"Lovell's men were badly outnumbered," Grandfather Wadsworth went on, "and nearly all of them were killed in the fight."

Grandfather Wadsworth's house stood on a huge piece of land in Maine, almost in the wilderness, where Indians had roamed just a few years before. The big wooden house was new then because Grandfather had built it after the American Revolution.

Grandfather Wadsworth had wonderful tales about his adventures in the Revolution. His grandsons begged him to tell, again and again, about how he had raised a company of minutemen, how he had been captured by the British soldiers, and how he had escaped from prison. His stories about the Revolution seemed very real because he still wore his three-cornered hat, ruffled shirt, knee britches, white stockings, and shoes with silver buckles.

But his experiences with the Indians were the most exciting for Henry. Grandfather knew endless stories about Indian chieftains and the tribes that once lived in Maine. Henry Longfellow never tired of hearing them.

"Tell the story of Lovell's Pond again," he begged.

The nearby forests were safe enough in 1812, when Henry Longfellow was five and his brother Stephen was seven, but the boys could pretend that dangers lurked there. After listening to Grandfather's stories, they could run through the woods and be minutemen or scout for Indians.

Henry liked best to roam through the forests alone. They were mysterious. The branches stirred and rustled and whispered. Indian maidens stepped out from behind trees. Stephen was too noisy to hear these imaginary sounds that Henry heard or to see the imaginary people that Henry saw.

Grandfather Longfellow was almost as interesting as Grandfather Wadsworth, and sometimes the boys spent part of their summer with him. His farm was near Portland, and there Stephen and Henry could play in the fresh hay, pick wild strawberries, and watch Grandmother Longfellow churn milk into butter. They could help with cornhusking or bring the cows home from pasture.

Most exciting of all for Henry was the blacksmith's shop that stood across the road from Grandfather Longfellow's house.

The blacksmith was a tall, strong man with big muscles in his arms, and he always turned around and smiled when he saw young Henry.

"Ho, there!" he would call. "Want to be a blacksmith someday?"

Henry nodded yes, but he wasn't sure he would ever be strong enough.

He stared into the fire while the blacksmith blew on it with his bellows and made it flame up around a piece of iron. Sparks flew all over the shop. The iron grew hot, as hot as the fire, until it turned red and soft. Then the blacksmith laid it on his anvil and hammered it into a horseshoe.

The dancing sparks and the glowing metal lived in Henry's memory as he raced away down the road.

But visits to Grandfather Wadsworth and Grandfather Longfellow were only for the summer. When vacation came to an end, Mrs. Longfellow gathered up her children—Stephen, Henry, four-year-old Betsy, and the infant Anne—and hurried them into a carriage with their packages to drive back to Portland, back to school, and back to Mr. Longfellow.

Imaginative Henry could find just as much adventure in Portland, because Portland was on the sea. As soon as their carriage stopped in front of the house, he jumped out and ran down to the wharves to watch the sailors—tall, strong sailors who strode back and forth. Some of them had rings in their ears. Some had bright red handkerchiefs tied around their heads. Some had thick black beards.

They came from everywhere, sailing into Portland Harbor in tall-masted ships. They laughed and shouted as they carried great kegs of molasses and sugar off the ships and stacked them on the shore. They laughed again as they loaded Maine lumber aboard the ship. Sometimes they waved to the small boy with brown hair and blue eyes as he sat upon the wharf, or they called greetings to him in languages he couldn't understand.

He liked to watch the black seawater, too, as it lapped against the soggy, wooden pier. The water smelled salty and fishy. If he sat there long enough, the water would come up, up, up, as the tide rose.

"Henry!" he heard his mother call, as he ran farther out on the pier and squatted down behind a keg.

It was no use. His mother found him and led him back.

"I want to watch the sea!" he protested. "I want to watch the tide come up."

"You're too small to be down here alone!" said his mother.

The sea was mysterious. It whispered just the way the pine trees in Grandfather's forest did, but Henry didn't have the words to explain.

Mrs. Longfellow held his hand as they walked back to the big brick house on Congress Street.

"May I go down and watch the ships again?" he asked.

"You won't have time," his mother told him. "Don't forget that school starts tomorrow."

Henry found Stephen sitting in a wide window seat in the front room, and he scrambled up beside his brother. If this were only the upstairs window, he would be able to see the ships from there, because the house wasn't far from the waterfront.

"Will we study about ships at public school?" Henry asked Stephen.

"Of course not!" said Stephen.

"About Indians, then?"

"You will learn to read and write in public school," said Mrs. Longfellow.

Henry had been to nursery school, but now that he was five he would go to the public school on Love Lane with his brother.

"Maybe they will teach us about ships and the sea," he sighed.

"You will have to learn spelling, writing, and arithmetic," Stephen told him.

Public school was even more disappointing than that, Henry found out the next day and in the days that followed. The boys in public school were rough, and they played hard.

"Do I have to go to school?" he would ask anxiously.

"The big boys always knock him down!" remarked Stephen.

"You have to learn to play with other boys," Mrs. Longfellow explained to Henry, and she made him go back each day.

Henry couldn't learn to play hard, rough games, and he couldn't learn to like public school. He grew more and more unhappy.

"I'll write to your father about it," his mother said at last.

Mr. Longfellow was a member of the Legislature of Massachusetts, which met in Boston.

Before Mr. Longfellow had time to write back and give any advice, Henry came home from public school angry and hurt and ready to cry.

"The teacher said I told a lie! I won't go back there again! I won't! I won't!"

At that, Mrs. Longfellow wrote another letter to Henry's father: "I think we should send the boys to a private academy."

"I quite agree," he wrote back. "And I think Portland Academy would be the best place for them."

Henry liked Portland Academy at once. Each day he ran the few blocks home, chattering like a squirrel about the classroom where boys sat on one side and girls on the other, about the boys who cut holes in the lift-up tops of their desks so they could peek through them at the girls. He brought home glowing reports about his progress.

All through the winter, the Longfellow boys went to Portland Academy. Often the snow was deep and the air biting cold.

In the evenings the family gathered around the big, round table, while Henry and Stephen did their lessons. If Mr. Longfellow was home, he sat there, too, and sometimes he read to his children. On Sundays he told them Bible stories.

If Mr. Longfellow was in Boston, Mrs. Longfellow sat at the big, round table with Stephen and Henry, writing letters to Mr. Longfellow, while the younger children laughed and cried and made a hubbub. By the time Henry was seven and Stephen nine, there were three other Longfellow children—Betsy, six; Anne, four; and Alex, four months.

"I am going to write to Papa," said Mrs. Longfellow one evening. "What do you want me to tell him?"

"I can write my own letter," said Stephen.

"Tell Papa," said Henry, "that I am writing at school—A, B, C— and send my love to him, and I hope he will bring me a drum."

"I think you should write your own letter, Henry," his mother told him.

So while his mother held his hand, Henry wrote:

Dear Papa: Anne wants a little Bible like Betsy's. Will you please buy her one, if you can find any in Boston? I have been to school all week . . . I wish you to buy me a drum.

Mr. Longfellow liked to receive letters from his children. When he finally came home, sailing from Boston to Portland, he strode into the house with his whole family gathered around him and his children clinging to him.

"Here is the Bible for Anne," he said gaily, holding up a package, "and here is a drum for Henry, with an eagle painted on it."

The children shouted and jumped around as presents came out for everybody.

Mr. Longfellow picked Henry up, tossed him into the air, and said, "After this, I want a letter from you every time I go away. I want to see how well you can write."

"I can write even better now," said Henry proudly.

CHAPTER 2
A SUMMER TRAGEDY

As winter wore on and spring weather melted the snow, the Longfellow boys tramped to school through March mud. When the muddy streets began to grow dry and dusty, Henry and Stephen grew excited. That meant school would close soon, and they could go visit their grandparents again.

"Are we going to Grandfather Wadsworth's?" asked Henry anxiously.

"Would you rather go there?" asked his mother.

He nodded his head hard. He wanted to hear more of those Indian stories that his grandfather told.

He was eight by then and able to understand the stories much better than when he had been only five.

And he wanted to run through the woods alone, find his imaginary Indian friends, and listen to the wind in the tall Maine pine trees.

The Longfellow children ran barefoot in the country. The minute they arrived, off came their shoes; then they darted off in every direction.

Henry was the first to return, limping badly and calling, "Mama, I've hurt my foot. I stepped on something."

"Let me see it," said Mrs. Longfellow. "I really shouldn't let you boys go barefoot."

Henry sat down while his mother washed the dirt from his foot and cleaned out the cut. She was always fixing somebody's cuts and bruises, so she didn't worry about it at first.

"May I go out again?" asked Henry.

"Yes, but don't get any more dirt into the cut."

The next day she looked at his foot again. It hadn't healed. The whole side of his foot had turned red and swollen.

"You'll have to stay in the house, Henry."

All day long she bathed his foot and watched over him, but he didn't get any better. His foot only grew more swollen, until his whole leg was swollen up and he couldn't move his toes.

Henry felt sick, and his head was hot. He just lay in bed and didn't even feel like sitting up.

Grandmother Wadsworth looked at the swollen foot and leg.

"We had better put some poultices on it," she said, and she sent Grandfather in the horse and carriage to fetch the doctor.

"Oh, dear!" sighed Mrs. Longfellow, when she realized how serious it was. "I wish Papa were here with us instead of in Boston."

The doctor applied some awful-smelling green salve. Still Henry didn't get any better, and still the leg stayed swollen.

"I'm afraid," the doctor said to Mrs. Longfellow, "that if the swelling doesn't go down, we will have to amputate his leg."

Mrs. Longfellow began to cry.

"Please don't tell Henry what the doctor said," she warned the other children.

Mournfully, Stephen, Anne, and Betsy sat by Henry's bed and watched him.

"Does it hurt very much?" asked Anne.

Henry nodded his head. He didn't even want to talk.

Grandfather Wadsworth sat there, too. So did Henry's mother, except when she went to the table to write a letter to Mr. Longfellow to let him know how Henry was getting along.

Henry was sick in bed for two weeks, until at last—nobody seemed to know just why—his leg began to get better. The swelling went down, his fever disappeared, and he felt like sitting up.

Everybody sighed with relief.

Summer was nearly over before Henry could get around. He had to walk on crutches for a while.

CHAPTER 3
The First Poem

H ENRY WAS able to go back to Portland Academy in the
fall, even though he didn't do much racing and running.
As he grew older, he grew quieter. He liked books, and
he liked to read. His writing improved each season until he could
send letters to his father that were clear and interesting.

His school work began to include Latin and Greek and
algebra, but Henry Longfellow found that he liked poetry best,
and he liked to memorize poetry. He learned whole songs by
heart when the family gathered around the piano and sang.

By the time he was twelve, his mother allowed him to wander
down to the Portland docks whenever school was out. The sailors
from all over the world told him tales of ships—pirate ships, tales
of storms at sea, and shipwrecks. He watched many a ship built
right there in Portland Harbor, watched the beam laid, watched
the skeleton fashioned of Maine timber, watched the mast
swung into place, and jumped up and down and shouted for joy
with the rest of the crowd when the great ship slid down into
the water.

The stories of ships and of sailors, the stories of lands far
away, the stories of Grandfather Wadsworth's Indians, all
began to jingle and dance in his imagination. Sometimes they
made patterns or fitted the tunes he sang and the poems he
memorized.

Henry Longfellow began to keep a copybook of his favorite poems. Into the copybook crept verses and jingles, rhymes and lines that he made up himself. He was becoming shy, and he kept his copybook a secret from almost everyone but his mother and his sister Anne.

Anne was nine, old enough to understand, when Henry was fourteen. Henry felt closer to her than to Stephen or Betsy. Stephen liked rougher play, and he didn't care for poetry. Betsy cared more about helping her mother with the younger children. There were eight Longfellow children in all, four boys and four girls.

There were plenty of books in the Longfellow home. Many of them contained poems that thrilled and excited Henry as he hunted through volume after volume.

Often when his father was at home, he helped Henry find his way among all those volumes. He would pull one down from a top shelf and say, "Here is a book that every educated man should know about."

Henry's ability to write was winning him honors at school, and his father was glad; but Mr. Longfellow didn't suspect that his son was dreaming about being a writer. Mr. Longfellow would not have approved of that.

Mrs. Longfellow was sympathetic, though, and Henry could confide all his dreams to her. She encouraged him, looked over his themes, helped him with new words, and read with him.

"What fun it would be," Henry thought, "if I didn't have to do anything but write and dream and write some more."

Henry wondered whether he should show his copybook to his Grandfather Wadsworth that summer. He wasn't sure. When he reached his Grandfather's house, he changed his mind.

"Tell me the story of Lovell's Pond again," he said to his Grandfather instead.

Grandfather laughed and stroked his beard. "You should know it by heart after all this time," he said.

Henry wanted to hear it again; he had a secret reason. Not even his sister Anne knew why Henry wanted to hear the tale again.

"Well," Grandfather Wadsworth began, "not far from this farm there's a pond, called Lovell's Pond. It is named for a brave man, Captain John Lovell, who died with his men in a terrible battle with the Indians."

The Longfellow children crept closer, all except Stephen, who announced he was too old for children's stories. But the younger brothers and sisters hadn't heard it too often, and to the youngest, the story was brand new.

"There were forty-six volunteers," Grandfather went on, "nearly a hundred years ago, combing these Maine woods for Indians. Well, right there at Lovell's Pond, they met a big band of Indians, and on that very spot they fought a terrible battle."

Henry's imagination filled in all the gaps in the story—the painted faces of the Indians, the tomahawks, the war whoops and yells echoing through the forests, slain warriors, and slain volunteers.

As soon as he was alone, he began to try out words on paper. How quiet it was in the forest now! Could there ever have been a battle here? Henry Longfellow wrote:

The war whoop is still, and the savage's yell
Has sunk into silence along the wild dell—

That was a poem! That was really a poem!

"I wonder," Henry dreamed with a new excitement, "if I could ever be a real poet someday?"

He worked hard on the rest of his poem about the Battle of Lovell's Pond, and when it was finished, he kept it hidden in his copybook.

How could he tell whether it was a real poem or not? If he showed it to his mother, she would praise him. If he showed it to his teachers, they would praise him. He decided not to show it to his father.

"Can you keep a secret?" he confided to his sister Anne.

Anne could always keep Henry's secrets.

"I've written a poem," he told her.

"Oh, Henry! Let me see it. Please let me see it."

He showed her the precious work, and after she had read it, she gazed at her wonderful brother.

"I think it's good, Henry! I think it's very good."

"Promise me you'll never tell anybody!" he warned her.

"I'll never tell; you know I'll never tell."

When the family returned to Portland in the fall and all the Longfellow children who were old enough were back in school, Henry still thought about his poem. If somebody read it, who didn't know that he had written it—and if that somebody thought it was really a poem—then he could be sure.

He had a plan. He knew how he would find out whether his poem was a poem.

He copied it on a fresh piece of paper, but when it came to signing his name, his heart sank. All he could write was "Henry."

After supper, when it was growing dark, when all the shops and offices were closed, Henry walked quietly away from the house on Congress Street until he came to Exchange Street. He knew where he was going. This was the great test.

He reached the printing shop of the town newspaper, the *Portland Gazette*. No one was around. Quickly he slipped his poem into the letter box and bolted up the street and home.

"Anne, Anne!" he whispered to his sister. "I did it! I gave my poem to the *Gazette*. Do you think they will print it? Do you think they will?"

The brother and sister waited breathlessly, and secretly, for the *Gazette* that came out only twice a week. The next issue arrived at the house on Friday.

Mr. Longfellow looked at the paper first. He sat down in his favorite chair and read slowly while Henry and Anne watched him with big eyes. Page after page! And not a word did he say.

At last he laid down the paper and left the room. Anne and Henry pounced upon it, turning the pages quickly to find Henry's poem. There it was! It *had* been published! It *was* a poem, really. They lay on their stomachs on the floor and read and read and read, "The Battle of Lovell's Pond."

> Cold, cold is the north wind and rude is the blast
> That sweeps like a hurricane loudly and fast,
> As it moans through the tall waving pines lone and drear,
> Sighs a requiem sad o'er the warrior's bier.

The war-whoop is still, and the savage's yell
Has sunk into silence along the wild dell;
The din of the battle, the tumult, is o'er,
And the war-clarion's voice is now heard no more.
The warriors that fought for their country, and bled,
Have sunk to their rest; the damp earth is their bed;
No stone tells the place where their ashes repose,
Nor points out the spot from the graves of their foes.
They died in their glory, surrounded by fame,
And Victory's loud trump their death did proclaim;
They are dead; but they live in each Patriot's breast,
And their names are engraven on honor's bright crest.

"I'm going to be a poet!" Henry assured Anne. "Just you wait and see."

That evening Henry went visiting at the house of his friend, Frederic Mellen. He didn't tell Frederic about the poem in the *Gazette*, but he did listen hopefully for any comment from the members of Frederic's family.

"By the way," said Mr. Mellen, as they sat around talking, "did you notice the poem in the *Gazette* today?"

Henry's heart skipped a beat.

"I think," Frederic's father went on, "that it was stiff, and every word of it was borrowed from other poems."

The whole world went dark for Henry Longfellow, and he didn't say another word for the rest of the evening.

On the way home, he walked along in the dark, under the big elm trees that lined the streets of Portland, depressed and discouraged.

He did tell Anne when he got home, making sure no one else could hear.

"I know how you feel, Henry," she said.

"He said it was borrowed from other poems."

"I think it was a good poem," Anne said. "If it wasn't a good poem, why would the newspaper print it?"

Henry was too crushed to think about it. He just went straight to his room and closed the door. When he was finally in bed, he buried his face in his pillow and cried and cried, until he fell asleep.

CHAPTER 4

COLLEGE

THERE WERE many more poems after that, in spite of the cruel remark. Henry was sure he wanted to be a poet, or at least some kind of writer. He found inspiration for new poems all around him—in the forests, in the sea, all over Portland. As the first snow began to fall, and the brooks and ponds began to freeze over, he wrote:

> Autumn has fled; and hoary Winter now
>   O'er hill and dale has spread his drear domain,
>   Covering with fleecy snow the fertile plain.
> With piercing storms the winds tempestuous blow
> And block the way. The streams refuse to flow—

There was more to it, full fourteen lines, and he signed it "H." He still didn't have the courage to sign his complete name. Suppose his father or his father's friend thought this one was borrowed, too?

The *Gazette* printed the second poem, and there were no more unkind comments.

"I'm sure," Henry confided to Anne, "that I can be a writer if I practice enough."

But even though Henry Longfellow was only fourteen, his family was talking about sending him to college. That meant more studying and less time for writing poetry.

"Of course, you and your brother will go to Bowdoin College," said Mr. Longfellow.

The two boys knew that when father spoke in that tone of voice he meant what he said.

But Stephen was bolder than Henry. "Why can't we go to Harvard, Papa?" he asked.

Stephen knew perfectly well why not, and so did Henry.

"Please remember," said Mr. Longfellow, "that your Grandfather Longfellow helped to found Bowdoin College, and I am a trustee."

Mrs. Longfellow was usually able to smooth things out, and she said, "Anyway, the first year you will be studying at home. You boys are too young to go away to college just yet."

So Stephen and Henry studied at Portland Academy another year, covering their freshman year subjects there. Even though Stephen was two years older than Henry, he started college the same year. Stephen was anxious to have school over with so that he could be a lawyer like his father. Henry was dreaming of other things.

At last, the day arrived when they would leave for college! Anne and Betsy helped their brothers pack and stood by the side of the road with their mother, watching the two boys get into the stagecoach to travel north to Bowdoin College in Brunswick, Maine.

"Goodbye! Goodbye!" everybody called.

Mrs. Longfellow was crying. This was the first time any of her children had gone away from home. Stephen and Henry were too excited about their adventure to feel sad.

"I'm going to meet a lot of new friends and have a lot of fun," dreamed Stephen.

"I'm going to read all the poetry by all the poets in the world," dreamed Henry.

Brunswick was a village on the Androscoggin River, and the college was at the edge of town. The stage horses trotted through town, along the dusty country road, and stopped in front of Bowdoin. There it was—much larger than Portland Academy! Bowdoin had four buildings, two of them made of brick, with green lawns all around. Young men wandered about on the lawns, or looked out of the windows, or stood talking in groups.

Stephen and Henry found they would not have as much freedom as they did at home. They had to be up at six every morning and go to chapel for prayers. Then they had classes almost all day, and they had to stay indoors evenings to study.

Henry didn't mind. He was doing what he wanted to do. At college, he found books, books, books, and chances to write and write. He found new friends who liked books and writing as much as he.

"Dear Parents," Henry wrote home, "I feel very well contented and am much pleased with college life. Many of the students are very agreeable, and, thus far, I have passed my time very pleasantly."

Soon boxes began to come from home—from Betsy and Anne—boxes of apples and pears and gingerbread, nuts, and cookies. Stephen and Henry and their college chums were always hungry.

Henry Longfellow was growing into an attractive young man, with fair skin and blue eyes and wavy brown hair. He was shy and gentle. His teachers liked him because he was so polite and cheerful and because he studied so carefully. His classmates liked him, too. But Henry's shyness kept him from making a great number of friends.

In the same class at Bowdoin was another shy young man, Nathaniel Hawthorne. He and Henry didn't become friends until years later.

Henry Longfellow was still in the Maine woods even though he was away at college. He liked to take long walks among the tall pine trees and think about the Indians that once wandered there. He was reading books about the Indians in college, books that told how they had lived and dressed and thought. He was beginning to understand them as people.

"I am learning to understand this persecuted race," he wrote home to his mother. "American Indians really have many beautiful customs and ideas and have been very badly treated by white people."

Many careful letters went home to his father and mother telling them exactly what he was doing. Henry wrote to his father about his lessons, his grades, his teachers, his friends. But his father was strict and formal, a stern lawyer; Henry couldn't tell him everything.

When he wrote to his mother, he could write about the things that mattered most—his reading, his poetry. He was writing more and more poetry, and sometimes he sent his poems home to his mother.

College went smoothly until Thanksgiving time rolled around. Then a feeling of homesickness set in. The Longfellow boys knew what fun Thanksgiving Day would be at home.

"I want to go home for Thanksgiving," said Stephen.

"So do I," agreed Henry.

They found that other young men at the college felt the same way, and most of them *were* going home for Thanksgiving.

"We usually just go home and surprise our families," the other fellows told them. "Why don't you do that?"

The Longfellow boys looked at each other. What an idea! To surprise the family! To drive up in front of the house in Portland and burst in through the front door just as Thanksgiving dinner was being put on the table! They would be surrounded by parents and grandparents, brothers and sisters, all laughing and happy to have them home.

They waited and schemed and planned for Thanksgiving Day. They counted up their money to make sure they had enough to rent the horse and carriage. On the great day, early in the morning, the air full of sharp frost, Stephen and Henry hurried to the stable.

"We want to rent a horse and carriage," they started to explain. The man shook his head.

"We have to have a carriage. We have to go home for Thanksgiving!"

"That's too bad," said the man who owned all the carriages. "But you see, all the boys at Bowdoin rent carriages to go home for Thanksgiving, and the last one has been taken. You should have reserved one in advance."

Crushed, sorrowful, and depressed, the Longfellow boys walked slowly back to school. No Thanksgiving dinner! No fun with the family! No fun at school either, because the campus was deserted. Everyone else had gone home.

One of the teachers discovered the two lonely men and took them to his house for dinner, but it wasn't the same. Henry especially wanted to see his mother and Anne and Betsy, and he wanted to talk to his father about his future.

Sad letters came from home in a few days. The family had really expected to be surprised.

"On Wednesday the children were all on tiptoe, and the window seats were filled every time a carriage passed. We waited dinner some time, and Ma kept some tidbits for you by the fire until night, and our tea was delayed to a late hour. You see, my dear children, how much we are all interested in everything that concerns you, and how tenderly we love you," wrote Mr. Longfellow.

CHAPTER 5
"*I Want to Be a Writer*"

T HERE WERE other opportunities to visit home during the three years at Bowdoin. There were winter holidays and long summers.

Each time that Henry came home, he planned to talk to his father about his writing, and each time he put it off.

"I could earn a living selling my poems," he dreamed. "I'm sure that I could."

Other papers besides the *Gazette* were publishing his poems—magazines in Philadelphia and Boston. Some of them even sent him money for them, and that was considerable for a young man still in school.

Each time another poem was published, Henry Longfellow felt less like becoming a lawyer.

When his senior year finally rolled around, he knew he must face facts with his father. He began to put hints into his letters home.

"I don't think I am suited to be a lawyer," he wrote in one letter.

By this time, his father was a member of the United States Congress. Mr. Longfellow was such a successful lawyer that he had been elected to high public office. He wanted his sons to have the same kind of success.

At last, Henry got up his courage and wrote to his father about the things closest to his heart: what he really wanted to be.

"After I graduate from Bowdoin, I should like to study for another year at Harvard. I should like to study great writers, and I should like to learn Italian and French so that I can read great writers in other languages."

Then he explained why: "You see, I want to be a writer. My whole soul burns most ardently for it."

He waited fearfully for his father's answer. His father had been reading some of his poems in the magazines. Maybe his father would change his mind about law. Maybe his mother would influence his father. Maybe he would have the chance after all.

The answer that came from Congressman Longfellow was crushing.

"Nobody earns a living at writing," stated his father firmly. "Please remember that we are not rich people, and you will have to support yourself. Being a lawyer is a very dignified way to earn a living. As for an extra year at college, I don't know whether I can afford it or not."

Henry had always listened to his father's advice, and he knew he would have to obey his father's wishes. He might have persuaded his father to let him study to be a minister or doctor, but they seemed even less interesting to Henry than being a lawyer. Henry loved his father, and he knew his father loved him. He knew, too, that there was only one way to convince his father that he could earn a living as a writer—and that would be to earn a living as a writer! Until such time, he would have to resign himself to being a lawyer.

"Perhaps you're right about the law," he wrote back to Mr. Longfellow. "I can do that to earn a living and write in my spare time."

Maybe someday he would be a successful writer, and then his father would have to say, "I guess I was wrong, Henry."

But among his college classmates, Henry Longfellow *was* a poet. Whenever they needed a poem for a special occasion, they called on Henry to write it. They were proud to know that one of their own members had poems appearing in magazines that were read all over the country.

Stephen had happier times in college and probably had a greater number of friends, but Henry was more deeply loved by those who knew him.

Henry was a better scholar than Stephen, too. By graduation time Henry stood third in a class of thirty-eight, and Stephen was way behind.

Eighteen-year-old Henry had done a lot of reading and thinking during his three years at college. He had discovered a lot of exciting and wonderful writers.

Among them was an American writer, Washington Irving. As Longfellow read Washington Irving's "Rip van Winkle" and "The Legend of Sleepy Hollow," his heart was captured. What was more wonderful about Irving, he had traveled in so many other countries. His book, *Tales of a Traveller*, came out when Henry Longfellow was a junior at Bowdoin. Washington Irving became Henry Longfellow's writer-hero.

But as Henry Longfellow read book after book, by this writer and that, he began to notice something that bothered him. Nearly all of the books were written by people in other countries. Many were written in England.

"Why don't we have more American writers?" he asked.

"America is a new country," one of his teachers explained. "We won our independence from England less than fifty years ago. When America is much older, then we'll have great American writers."

Henry pondered and thought. There ought to be more American writers, like Washington Irving, and he—Henry Longfellow—decided that he was going to be one of them.

Graduation day was almost at hand. Since Henry stood so high in his class, he was writing a paper for the occasion.

When he read his paper before the Class of 1825, and before all the friends and relatives who had traveled to the campus for graduation, his subject was, "Our Native Writers."

And that was not all. On the following day, Henry Longfellow met with his classmates one more time and read them a farewell poem.

CHAPTER 6

LANDS BEYOND THE SEA

WITHOUT A word to his father or to anyone else, Henry Longfellow wrote a secret letter to the editor of one of the magazines that had been buying his poetry. He wanted a job, he explained politely. He wanted to "breathe a little while a literary atmosphere."

Even though he had promised his father that he would study law, Henry still hoped to avoid it somehow.

The editor crushed the young man with the same advice his father had given him: "It is impossible to earn a living in America as a writer."

Mr. Longfellow had said that Henry could study at Harvard before beginning his law work, but that was just putting it off a year.

"Remember," he said to Henry, "when you finish your year at Harvard, you will have to study law."

But the professors at Bowdoin had been watching young Longfellow, too. Before he could start his year at Harvard, his father returned one day from a trustees' meeting at Bowdoin and said, "Bowdoin wants you to return there and teach. There is a new position open. They need a professor of modern languages— someone to teach French, Spanish, Italian, and maybe German."

Henry Longfellow became excited over that. They would hold the job for him while he went to Europe to learn a few languages.

"Maybe Papa will forget about the law," he confided to Anne and Betsy.

His father surprised him.

"Of course, you can go to Europe to study for a year or two," said Mr. Longfellow. "But you can't sail until next spring, so in the meantime, you can study law in my office."

The romantic young man, with poetry in his heart, his head full of dreams of traveling like his writer-hero Washington Irving, tried his best to keep his mind on his father's law books. The law office was one of the front rooms of the house on Congress Street in Portland.

"Perhaps your brother Stephen and some of your friends can study law with you," said Mr. Longfellow.

That was a mistake. Mr. Longfellow couldn't be there to look after them, and Henry and his friends had more fun than work for a few months. Anyone walking past the house could hear them laughing and talking and carrying on at a great rate. Nobody learned very much law. Sometimes Henry would go off into a corner by himself and write verse.

The waiting was over at last, and the whole family rushed around getting Henry ready for his journey. Mrs. Longfellow was most worried about what he should wear. She talked to everybody she knew who had ever been to Europe. Stephen was off to his own affairs and not worried about Henry at all. Anne and Betsy chattered about the letters they would receive from faraway places.

"Can you write to us every day, Henry?"

"Of course not!" said Mrs. Longfellow. "Henry is going abroad to study. He can't spend all of his time writing letters."

Alex, Mary, Ellen, and Samuel were too young to be helpful, but they joined in the commotion and ran up and down stairs whenever anyone else did.

Everybody gave a lot of advice, especially Mr. Longfellow's friends. Some said, "Go to Italy and study Italian." Others said, "Go to Germany and study German."

Henry had a dream of his own. His hero, Washington Irving, was in Spain.

"What do you think of the idea of going to Spain?" he asked his father cautiously.

"I think it would be a good idea to go to Spain and learn some Spanish," was the answer.

Before nineteen-year-old Henry went aboard the sailing ship in New York, one more thing happened to add to his dreams and excitement. A publisher in Philadelphia was bringing out a large book of poems, and he wanted some of Henry's poems for the book.

"I *can* write!" Henry gasped. "I *am* going to be a writer someday!" And he sent the publisher three brand-new poems.

Then off to Europe—the land beyond the seas—the faraway land of storybooks. After thirty days at sea, Henry Longfellow reached the coast of France.

"I have reached the shores of the Old World," he wrote to his mother, and he told her that the voyage had been safe.

"The country folk here wear wooden shoes full of feet and straw," he wrote to Stephen.

He was headed for Paris, which was inland, and he wrote his sisters a long letter about the carriage, or diligence, in which he rode to Paris. A man on horseback galloped alongside the carriage, cracking his whip over the horses' heads to make them trot faster, he explained; and the roads were dusty.

As soon as he reached Paris, he wrote to his father and promised him that he would study hard.

Henry Longfellow was not alone in Paris. He and six other young men were living at the home of Madame Potel. She decided that she was the mother of them all, and she sat at the head of the dinner table each evening making all the young men speak French.

"You have come to France to learn to speak French," she told them firmly. "I must hear French."

It was hard to do, but they knew it was good for them. They knew, too, that if they spoke English or any other language, Madame Potel would make them pay a coin.

Paris was hot and noisy in the summertime, and Henry Longfellow had arrived just as the summer was starting. His classes at the University of Paris would not begin until the fall. Why not see the country meanwhile?

He packed a knapsack and started out on foot to see the French countryside. He wandered along country roads, past golden-yellow wheat fields sprinkled with red poppies. He saw French villages and towns, and he met the farm folk. If he liked a town, he stayed there awhile. He saw forests and woods that reminded him of the woods in Maine.

This was a new kind of freedom for Henry Longfellow. He had never been really far from home before. Here he could almost do as he pleased.

He traveled all summer making friends with everybody.

"It's easy to learn to speak French here," he wrote home to his family. "The French are always talking."

When the air began to feel cool and crisp enough for study, he returned to Paris and settled down to his classes at the university.

His father was keeping track of him.

"Your trip is costing me a great deal more than I expected," Mr. Longfellow reminded Henry. "I hope you are working and not wasting your time."

Henry thought guiltily about the time he had wasted all summer. So he tried to make up for it by studying hard all winter. When spring returned, though, he began to dream of all the strange places he wanted to see.

Spain! Wintertime in Paris was cold and gloomy, but summer in Spain would be sunny and warm.

"I am on my way to Spain!" Henry wrote back to Portland. Mail took so long to cross the ocean that he was in Spain before the letter reached his family.

He traveled south in another diligence, down through France and across the mountains. Henry began to see a wonderland, a land he would never forget. He hadn't written much lately. Spain made him remember that he was a poet.

White hamlets hidden in fields of wheat,
    White cities slumbering by the sea,
White sunshine flooding square and street,
Dark mountain ranges, at whose feet
The river beds are dry with heat—
    All was a dream to me.

He saw Moorish mosques, farmers leading donkeys with panniers on their saddles, windmills, groves of dark-green olive trees, orange orchards, and castles on hilltops. At last he reached the city of Madrid, in the center of Spain. He had never seen a city like this one before. It was the most beautiful city in the world, he was sure. Rows of buildings gleamed white in the sun, each one a palace.

Harder to study here! Too many things to do and too many places to see—in Madrid and all over Spain! Henry Longfellow was still only nineteen. He was too young to settle down.

"I'll do as much studying as I can," he promised his father.

Henry Longfellow had a real talent for languages, and he was quickly learning to speak Spanish.

The day he met Washington Irving was Henry Longfellow's greatest day in Spain.

The author of "Rip van Winkle" was hard at work at his desk in Madrid. To Henry Longfellow he had a "most beautiful countenance," with dark hair and a beard that was turning gray. Washington Irving was jovial and friendly, and he nodded and smiled at his young visitor.

"How do you do, Mr. Irving," said the young man who was so full of poetry that he hoped to write.

"Please sit down and wait a moment," said Mr. Irving. "I must finish this sentence."

He finished writing his sentence and then sat back in his chair to talk to Henry Longfellow.

"I am writing the life of Christopher Columbus," said Washington Irving. "I must work long hours every day, because the publisher is waiting for the book. I start every morning at six o'clock and work all day long."

Henry felt ashamed of himself. He knew that he, too, ought to be working hard instead of rambling around the country.

Mr. Irving liked Henry, and Henry liked Mr. Irving. Washington Irving took the young man under his wing. He gave him advice about writing, and he introduced him to other interesting people in Spain.

Henry could not stay in Spain forever. He must move on and see other countries. What about Italy? The students at Bowdoin might want him to teach them some Italian when he returned.

An unexpected letter from home made him want to go straight to Germany and omit Italy altogether. It was from a boy named Ned Preble who had gone to Portland Academy with Henry and Stephen Longfellow.

"My family is letting me study abroad," wrote Ned Preble. "And I am going to the University of Göttingen in Germany. Can't you come there, too? We could room together."

An old, familiar friend, after being away from home so long! Someone his own age to whom he could tell *all* of his adventures! That would be almost as good as going home, if he could find someone from Portland in Europe.

Or, why not just go home? He'd been traveling in foreign countries enough, and he felt homesick. It would be fun to wander through the woods of Maine, or walk along the streets of Portland, or watch the sailing ships come and go in the harbor.

His family could tell from his letters how homesick he was.

"Don't be discouraged," his father wrote him. "Remember there is a good job waiting for you at Bowdoin. As long as you are in Europe you may as well learn all you can. Why not go on to Italy and then to Germany?"

Henry did as he was told. He usually did as his father wished. But he wrote home again. "Tell Mama and all the family that before I left them I did not know how much I loved them."

So, after saying goodbye to Washington Irving and other friends in Spain, Henry Longfellow traveled on—alone.

The first Italian city he visited was Genoa, and he didn't find it very interesting, in spite of all its beauty. From there he went on southward to Florence. Might as well stay in Florence to study Italian as anywhere else, he decided. Florence was a beautiful city, too. After a few weeks, though, Henry moved on, traveling still farther south to the city of Rome.

He found a room with a family named Persiani. They turned out to be charming people and merry company for the solitary young man. The daughters were talented; one could play the harp, and another could sing and play the piano. Rome was going to be attractive after all, now that he had friends. And there were the Pantheon, the Colosseum, catacombs, theatres, and carnivals.

"You can judge from my long residence in Italy that I am much pleased with it. Its language is very beautiful," he reported to his family.

In Italy Longfellow met another young American student, from Rhode Island, who became his lifelong friend. George Washington Greene was stopping at the same house in Rome. Longfellow and he had met on the journey from France to Genoa, and they were overjoyed to meet again in Rome. Greene was the grandson of the famous General Nathanael Greene, who had fought so bravely with General George Washington in the American Revolution. The two young men often went sightseeing together.

Longfellow learned to love Italy nearly as much as Spain, and he stayed there for almost a year. Italian was a beautiful language. As soon as he was able to read in Italian, he discovered the works of Italian poets. He was really beginning to enjoy languages. His job at Bowdoin was going to be interesting.

Then came the news from home—bad news. A letter from his father.

"I'm afraid Bowdoin College has changed its mind. After we've spent so much money training you, and after you've spent so much time in Europe, Bowdoin College has decided that they don't want you as a professor after all. They think you are too young. Would you be willing to be an instructor at Bowdoin? The salary would be much lower."

Angry, hurt, his hopes dashed! Henry Longfellow didn't know what he was doing for a little while. Would he have to be a lawyer? He rushed around his room, throwing his things into his suitcase, trying to choke back the tears. Even if it did mean he would have to be a lawyer, he could not accept such an insult from Bowdoin.

He sat down with pen and paper.

"My dear Father. They say I am too young! Were they not aware of this three years ago? I will certainly *not* accept a less important job for a lower salary."

"Think it over more carefully," his father wrote back. "As long as you are in Europe, you may as well go on to Germany and learn to speak and read German. Remember that this is what some of my friends advised. After all, you *are* very young."

Again Henry did as his father told him. He said goodbye to the Persianis and set out for Germany, to the city of Göttingen and Ned Preble.

"What took you so long to get here?" Ned Preble asked when Henry Longfellow finally arrived.

"My father wanted me to go to Italy first," Henry explained.

Ned's room was a real student's room with two long swords hung crisscross on the wall. And when Ned took Henry out to show him the town and introduce him to all his friends, Göttingen turned out to be very different from Italy or Spain. Henry saw young men in frock coats and buckskin breeches, peasant boys in blue smocks wearing round black caps on their heads and smoking long pipes. Peasant girls carried great baskets of vegetables on their backs. The houses had steep, pointed roofs.

The university was the most important thing in Göttingen, and it seemed that everybody in town was either a professor, a student, or a tradesman.

At first, Henry was lost among the hundreds of young men. He couldn't converse with them until he learned German, so he concentrated on that.

He couldn't forget his disappointment, though. He couldn't forget that Bowdoin thought he was "too young." They were mistaken! Hadn't he already had some of his poetry published? Someday maybe he would be as famous as Washington Irving. Then what would Bowdoin have to say for itself?

He closed his eyes and began to dream of Washington Irving. He dreamed about writing his own book, many of his own books.

"I am planning to write a book of my own," Henry confided to his father. "I am going to write about my travels in France and Spain and Italy and Germany."

He discovered that he liked German as much as he had Italian, and he liked to read books written in German. There was a huge library in the city, and after a while the librarian let him take books to his room.

"May I stay in Germany a little longer than we planned?" he wrote to his father.

He had been away from home for three years, but his father let him remain longer.

After a few months, though, Mr. Longfellow had to change his mind about allowing Henry to stay in Germany.

"I think you had better think about coming home soon, Henry. Your sister Betsy is sick, and the doctor says she may never get well."

That gave Henry a new case of homesickness. Each letter that came from home—from Anne, from his mother, from Stephen—made him more homesick. He wanted to see Betsy. He wanted to talk to her about all his travels and adventures. Maybe he could cheer her up so she would get better.

He packed his things, said goodbye to his friends in Germany, and started for home. He had to go to France to board a ship.

Here another letter reached him that sent his spirit still lower. He opened it eagerly, but let it drop from his fingers.

Betsy had died—before he could even get home to see her.

CHAPTER 7

HENRY LONGFELLOW AND MARY POTTER

HENRY LONGFELLOW returned to a sorrowful family. His mother and father were solemn and talked very little. Even carefree Stephen was more serious than usual. It was Anne, though, who talked to Henry about Betsy when they were alone.

Henry hardly knew his younger brothers and sisters, because they had had more than three years to grow while he was away. Samuel, the baby, was ten years old.

Mr. Longfellow did have a long conversation with Henry about the position in Bowdoin. They had discussed it carefully in their letters, too, while Henry was still in Germany. Henry's anger had cooled, and his father advised him to take the less important job that Bowdoin offered.

"As long as you don't want to be a lawyer or doctor or minister," said Mr. Longfellow, "perhaps you may like teaching. Why not take this post for the time being? It will give you experience."

"I can't accept such a cut in salary after you spent so much money educating me in Europe for three years," Henry protested.

Bowdoin College really wanted Henry Longfellow on its staff, and a compromise was worked out. He could be college librarian, too, and that would add to his salary.

So Henry accepted the compromise and agreed to teach at Bowdoin in the fall. He spent the rest of the summer in Portland with his family.

Everyone in Portland noticed the interesting young Henry Longfellow. He seemed more handsome than when he had gone away. He was much more mature and dignified. He had a way of standing straight and walking with a long stride. It was clear that he knew a great deal. And why not? Hadn't Henry Longfellow studied abroad for three years?

And how well he dressed! His dark brown jacket fitted him around the waist without a wrinkle, its long tails cut to perfection. His light-colored pantaloons with the strap that reached under the foot were the very latest fashion. He carried his high hat, his gloves, and his walking stick like a perfect gentleman.

The first Sunday morning that Henry went to church with his family, he could feel everybody watching him. He was still a shy fellow, in spite of all his traveling, and for a few minutes, he was uncomfortable. Only for a few minutes, though.

Across the aisle sat a young lady, her dark curls showing under a big lacy hat. She was wearing a white organdy dress that came down to her ankles, and she had a wide ribbon sash tied around her waist. She turned her head and looked at Henry, and he saw her blue eyes.

Henry nudged Anne. "Who is that?" he whispered.

"That's Mary Potter. Don't you remember her? She used to go to Portland Academy when you did."

Henry didn't hear the sermon that Sunday morning. He just sat and watched Mary Potter.

As soon as church was out, he said to Anne, "You must come visiting with me this very afternoon at the Potters."

Anne laughed and agreed.

All the rest of the summer, Henry Longfellow called on Mary Potter, until at last he had to go to Bowdoin College in Brunswick to start teaching. Mary promised to write him, and whenever he wrote to her, he sent the letter to Anne, who took it secretly to Mary. Mary's father was strict.

His first year at Bowdoin was dull and disappointing and full of unpleasant work. He taught classes in Spanish and French; he helped watch over the boys in the dormitory; he spent part of every day in the library; he spent his evenings correcting piles of papers. By the time his day ended, he had little energy left to write poetry.

But there were letters to Mary Potter and letters from Mary Potter. And there were holidays home with Mary Potter. After two years at Bowdoin, Henry Longfellow wrote to Mary's father, asking permission to marry her.

Henry Longfellow and Mary Potter were married in September 1831. They went back to Brunswick together and moved into a house not far from the college where Henry taught.

With Mary to encourage him and look after him, Henry began to feel really happy and ambitious. He remembered once more that he wanted to be a writer.

He settled down to hard work, getting up at five in the morning to study and read before he went to his classes, and working late into the evening.

"What about the book of your travels in Europe that you said you wanted to write?" Mary asked him.

Hopefully, Henry Longfellow once again took out his notes on his travels in Spain, Italy, and Germany. He had already written some of the book. Now he settled down to work in earnest. *Outre-Mer* he decided he would call it, meaning, "Beyond the Seas."

The first chapter had already been published in a magazine. Why not others? Soon a second chapter appeared. A few months later, out came a third. Mary and he were both excited about it. Maybe this would be the end of drudgery in Bowdoin.

Henry still hoped he would be able to win his father over, and he sent him some of the chapters to read.

"When it comes out in book form," Henry explained, "I'm going to call it *Outre-Mer*."

"I don't like the title," was all his father had to say. "And I think you will have a hard time finding a publisher."

Henry had learned not to let his father's attitude discourage him. When the book was a success, his father would change his mind quickly enough.

He continued to work on new chapters of *Outre-Mer*, but they came along slowly. His teaching required a great deal of him, even though he was more interested in his writing.

"I wish I could find a more interesting job than teaching in Bowdoin," he said to Mary more than once.

She agreed. For a man who had traveled all over Europe and studied in so many different places and spoke other languages so well, Bowdoin seemed slow and stuffy.

Henry Longfellow did find a publisher for *Outre-Mer*, and the book came out in 1833. The reviews and comments in the newspapers and magazines about *Outre-Mer* were so favorable that Henry and Mary were thrilled, and Henry promptly began to write a second volume of his travels.

"Now, Henry," said Mary, "you must look around for a new job, something worthy of you."

He had been at Bowdoin five years. He wrote letters here and there, inquiring about positions, but nothing turned up. He had to stay in Bowdoin for a sixth year.

In December of that year, things began to change for the better. Harvard University offered him a position teaching languages, and the salary was much higher than the one Bowdoin was paying him.

He and Mary were overjoyed. So was his family in Portland.

"If you would like to take some time off," said the letter from Harvard, "to go to Europe and study, we will hold the job for you."

Another chance to travel! Another chance to go abroad!

"I'm afraid to go," said Mary. "I've never been to Europe."

Henry would not hear of her staying home.

"You'll like it once you're there," he promised her. "Traveling with you will be much more pleasant than traveling alone."

They closed up their house and packed all their things into boxes to be stored away. When they came back, they would be living in a different city.

Longfellow planned to go to Germany by way of England and Sweden, and he and Mary had a lot of fun exploring new places together. In England, Longfellow was thrilled to meet other writers, like Thomas Carlyle, and he arranged for the publication of his *Outre-Mer* in England.

Henry and Mary stopped in Sweden all summer, because it was cool there, and because Henry wanted to study the Swedish language.

At the end of the summer, they traveled down to Holland. Mary was beginning to look as though she had had enough of strange countries and all the discomforts of travel.

"I feel tired, Henry," she said.

"We can stop here for a while before we go on to Germany," he told her. "You need a rest."

Mary was more than tired. She was ill, and she became worse. In a panic, Henry sent for a doctor.

"She had better stay in bed," said the doctor.

She grew worse. She had a fever at times, and she ached with rheumatism.

The Longfellow family and the Potter family back in Portland began to receive sorrowful letters from Henry.

"I am much grieved to say that Mary is not well today," he reported to his father. "She is very feeble, and the doctor says her condition is dangerous."

By the middle of November, Henry realized that Mary would never be well again, and he sat by her bedside all day long.

"My poor Mary is worse today. Sinking, sinking—"

After another week, Mary Longfellow closed her eyes to sleep and never opened them again, and Henry Longfellow had to write the saddest letter of his life:

"This morning, between one and two o'clock, my Mary, my beloved Mary, ceased to breathe. She is now, I trust, a Saint in Heaven. Would that I were with her."

A crushed and heartbroken Henry Longfellow left Holland and went on to Germany. He felt lost and dazed with no way to turn. He went to the city of Heidelberg where he thought he would try to study. Sometimes he wandered into a darkened church and sat down alone. Sometimes he went out into the country and took long walks through the forests.

"Every day makes me more conscious of the loss I have suffered in Mary's death; and when I think how gentle and affectionate and good she was, every moment of her life, even to the last, and that she will be no more with me in this world—the sense of my bereavement is deep and unutterable."

During the winter months, he found that work was the best cure for sorrow. He studied hard and read a great many books, especially by German poets.

In the spring he decided to take a vacation in the high mountains of Switzerland. He traveled along, seeing steep hillsides, beautiful waterfalls, icy glaciers and deep lakes, Swiss cottages, and terraced gardens. But he was traveling alone, and Henry Longfellow no longer liked to do that. It would have been much more fun with Mary.

When he reached the Swiss lake of Thun, he struck up a friendship with a man from Boston named Appleton. That helped a little, but they were traveling different ways and soon parted. They met again at Interlaken, where Mr. Appleton and his two daughters, Mary and Fanny, were spending their vacation. They were delighted to meet Henry Longfellow because they had read his book, *Outre-Mer*.

Fanny Appleton was only seventeen and joyous and full of fun. She had sparkling black eyes and reddish-brown hair. She took charge of the lonely, sorrowful, and handsome young writer. She and Henry went on carriage drives and boat trips. They went on long walks together, and Fanny usually carried her sketchbook. Whenever they stopped to rest, Henry watched as she drew pencil pictures of the village of Interlaken and the lake and the tall, snow-covered mountains in the background—or perhaps pictures of an old castle, a cottage, or the hotel where they were staying.

Henry Longfellow was beginning to feel like himself again and beginning to feel deeply interested in Fanny Appleton.

At the end of three weeks, he had to leave Switzerland and return to Harvard and his new teaching position. The Appletons were staying in Switzerland a while longer.

They were all going to see each other again, though, because Henry was going to Cambridge on one side of the Charles River, and the Appletons lived in Boston on the other side of the river.

"You must come and call on us in Boston as soon as we return," they made him promise.

CHAPTER 8

CRAIGIE HOUSE

C AMBRIDGE WAS a quiet village when Longfellow went to live there in 1836. Huge trees shaded the streets, and the Charles River wound sleepily by.

Henry Longfellow went about in search of rooms. After trying several places, he called on Mrs. Craigie. Her large and beautiful two-story house on Brattle Street stood far back from the road, surrounded by giant elms, and just a short walk from Harvard where he would be teaching.

Mrs. Craigie at first said "no" to the young man looking for lodgings; she thought him a bit too merry-looking and altogether too fashionable. But when he explained that he was a professor and an author—the man who had written *Outre-Mer*—she changed her mind and invited him in.

"I've read your book," she said proudly, as she led him up the carpeted staircase with its carved, white banister. She showed him the two front rooms.

"General George Washington once occupied these very rooms," she told him, "and Mrs. Washington served tea in the downstairs parlor."

He looked out the front window and saw wide, green fields, and beyond them was the Charles River curving along. He began at once to love Craigie House and all of Cambridge.

He found that his work and friends at Harvard University were as pleasant as his big, airy rooms at Craigie House. Charles

Sumner was teaching in the Harvard Law School. He and Longfellow soon became close friends. Ralph Waldo Emerson was living in nearby Concord and giving lectures in Boston. Henry Longfellow often went to hear him speak, and they, too, became friends.

Longfellow had more leisure time at Harvard than he had had at Bowdoin. He had time to write, time to read his favorite German and Italian poets, and time to remember Fanny Appleton.

As soon as the Appletons returned from Switzerland, Henry Longfellow could be seen walking across the bridge to Boston to call on them. An hourly stage ran to Boston that he could ride in, if he was in a hurry. Often he strolled in Boston Common with Mary and Fanny Appleton.

He called at other fashionable homes in Boston, too, because the polite and gentle Mr. Longfellow was becoming very popular. But he never called so often anywhere as at the Appletons.

Mr. Longfellow was becoming very much aware of one fact: he was in love with Fanny Appleton.

As he sat in his room at Craigie House thinking about her, he began to remember once more that he wanted to be a poet, that he really was a poet.

> Gorgeous flowerets in the sunlight shining,
>   Blossoms flaunting in the eye of day,

he began. Of course, the poem was for Fanny Appleton. When it was finished, Henry Longfellow felt as afraid to show it to her as he had felt about his first poem. He finally bought a bouquet of flowers, tucked the poem inside, and hurried across the bridge to Boston. He was going to tell Fanny that he loved her, and he was going to ask her to marry him! As soon as they were married and living in Cambridge, he would be the happiest man in the world.

That was his dream, but it was not Fanny's. The beautiful Miss Fanny Appleton said "no" to the poet.

Crushed and disappointed, Mr. Longfellow had a new kind of sorrow. He could still visit with the Appletons. He could still meet Fanny and Mary on Boston Common. But he could not marry beautiful Fanny.

Perhaps she thought he wasn't important enough. Perhaps her family thought she was too young to marry. She was only eighteen.

He wasn't going to give up. He went on teaching at Harvard, visiting with friends and neighbors in Cambridge and Boston, and writing, writing, writing, in his spare time.

"I hope this fine new appointment at Harvard will make you forget your silly ideas about writing," his father had said.

His father was mistaken, as usual. Henry sometimes sat at his desk in Craigie House with his head in his hands, brooding, searching for words to express his feelings. Life seemed so empty, so mournful; and yet it ought not to be.

> Tell me not, in mournful numbers,
>   Life is but an empty dream!
> For the soul is dead that slumbers,
>   And things are not what they seem.

That was how his poem, "A Psalm of Life," began. He worked on it long hours, verse after verse, and he knew it was a real inspiration.

> Life is real! Life is earnest!
>   And the grave is not its goal;
> Dust thou art, to dust returnest,
>   Was not spoken of the soul.

It was published in the *Knickerbocker Magazine*, and everyone became excited about it. Young and old read it and loved it and memorized it.

Henry Longfellow, the poet, was beginning to come into his own. He was only thirty-one years old—plenty of time left in which to be a successful writer.

He and Nathaniel Hawthorne, of Salem, Massachusetts, finally became better acquainted. They had both been too shy at Bowdoin, but one day Hawthorne wrote Longfellow at Harvard.

"We were not well acquainted in college," Hawthorne wrote, "but perhaps you remember me. I have read your *Outre-Mer* and think it is excellent. Have you read my book, *Twice-Told Tales*?"

"Your book is excellent. It comes from the hand of a man of genius. You are a poet at heart," Longfellow wrote back.

One letter led to another until the two important American writers were friends, visiting back and forth between Salem and Cambridge.

Longfellow still corresponded with his friend, George Washington Greene, who was now United States consul at Rome, Italy.

Through it all, though, Henry Longfellow was still in love with Fanny Appleton, no matter how hard he tried to forget. He had known her for more than two years. How to convince her? How to persuade her to marry him?

In the midst of his teaching, his verse writing, his dreaming, his brooding, he had another idea: a book, a novel that would tell the story of his love for Fanny Appleton!

He worked all winter on the novel, and the next summer it was published. *Hyperion* was its title.

Those who knew Longfellow knew what the story meant the minute they read the book. The hero of the book was Henry Longfellow with a different name. The heroine of the book was Fanny Appleton with a different name. It described her exactly as she was. How tongues wagged! How people gossiped and talked!

Henry's hopes ran high when he saw how successful his book was and how many copies sold. If his beautiful Fanny recognized herself when she read the book, maybe she would realize how deeply he loved her. Maybe she would change her "no" to "yes" and marry him.

Miss Fanny recognized herself quickly enough.

She also heard the gossip and talk that the book was causing—about her. She soon made it clear to the rash Mr. Longfellow that he need not call on her again.

That was the end, Longfellow knew. He had made a terrible blunder.

Not that long after that, his first book of poems was published. It included "A Psalm of Life." At least his dream of becoming a poet was coming true. His fame was spreading as more people read his novel and verse.

His family was proud of him. To his mother and his father and brothers and sisters, he was *their* Henry. His students at Harvard were proud of him. He was *their* Professor Longfellow. After his book of poems was published, young Harvard men listened more closely when Professor Longfellow talked to them about the poets of Germany and Italy.

In another two years, a second volume of Henry Longfellow's verse came out, and his admirers rushed to buy it. In this new book were more poems that would be remembered forever: "The Skeleton in Armor," "The Wreck of the Hesperus," and "The Village Blacksmith."

How everyone loved "The Village Blacksmith"! Families read it around their fireplaces in the evening. School children memorized it and recited it.

Under a spreading chestnut tree
  The village smithy stands;
The smith, a mighty man is he,
  With large and sinewy hands;
And the muscles of his brawny arms
  Are strong as iron bands.
His hair is crisp, and black, and long,
  His face is like the tan;
His brow is wet with honest sweat,
  He earns whate'er he can,
And looks the whole world in the face,
  For he owes not any man.
Week in, week out, from morn till night,
  You can hear his bellows blow;
You can hear him swing his heavy sledge,
  With measured beat and slow,
Like a sexton ringing the village bell,
  When the evening sun is low.
And children coming home from school
  Look in at the open door;
They love to see the flaming forge,
  And hear the bellows roar,
And catch the burning sparks that fly
  Like chaff from a threshing floor.
He goes on Sunday to the church,
  And sits among his boys;
He hears the parson pray and preach,
  He hears his daughter's voice,
Singing in the village choir,
  And it makes his heart rejoice.
It sounds to him like her mother's voice,
  Singing in Paradise!
He needs must think of her once more,
  How in the grave she lies;

And with his hard, rough hand he wipes
  A tear out of his eyes.
Toiling,—rejoicing,—sorrowing,
  Onward through life he goes;
Each morning sees some task begin,
  Each evening sees it close;
Something attempted, something done,
  Has earned a night's repose.
Thanks, thanks to thee, my worthy friend,
  For the lesson thou hast taught!
Thus at the flaming forge of life
  Our fortunes must be wrought;
Thus on its sounding anvil shaped
  Each burning deed and thought.

Longfellow was giving more happiness to others than he could give to himself. He was still deeply unhappy about Fanny Appleton. Whenever he went to parties and meetings and listened to praises about his poetry, he thought of Miss Fanny. Other young ladies in Cambridge and Boston simply did not interest him.

He began to feel tired and listless. He had been working very hard for several years, teaching and writing, and he decided that he needed a rest, a real rest away from it all.

"I am planning a long vacation," he told one of his friends, "a trip to Europe."

Off he went—to England and Germany to look up old friends and meet new ones. He spent the whole summer abroad and did not come back until the late fall.

As he strolled around on the deck of the ship that was bringing him back across the ocean, the sharp sea air made him feel like working again.

"I ought to be doing some writing," he decided.

He dreamed and mused about home. What was going on there? What were people most interested in in 1842? His friends were probably still arguing about slavery. Charles Sumner had been making speeches against slavery for years. Charles Sumner, Ralph Waldo Emerson, John Greenleaf Whittier, Henry Longfellow—were all opposed to slavery and wanted it abolished.

"Longfellow, why don't you write some poems against slavery?" Charles Sumner often said. "Everybody reads your poetry, and you could influence a lot of people."

Longfellow was too gentle to like any kind of argument, but he began to reflect. He was a Puritan; he was trained to be kindly; the mere thought of owning a person like a piece of furniture made him unhappy. As for whipping a slave—

Quietly, during the long days at sea, Henry Longfellow began to write a set of poems on slavery, seven in all.

When he reached home and published his poems on slavery, his friends were surprised.

"I never expected you to write anything political," said Hawthorne.

"Oh, I'm not getting into politics," said Longfellow. "I really wrote them because I felt disturbed about slavery—and to please Charles Sumner."

He was home. He felt rested. He was busy working again. But the lonely professor was still in love with Fanny Appleton. Practically everyone in Cambridge and Boston and Portland knew why the handsome, stylishly dressed poet looked so mournful at times. It was because of that indifferent young Boston lady! By now she was twenty-four, and she seemed to grow more beautiful every year.

"I really am tired of this," said a Cambridge lady one day. "Henry Longfellow and Fanny Appleton would make an ideal couple. I am going to arrange it."

So the lady gave a party on a warm April evening when the windows of her large, lovely house could be opened to the garden. She invited dozens of persons—and Henry Longfellow and Fanny Appleton.

The poet accepted the invitation because he liked society. As he strolled from room to room, talking to this one and that, he decided it was a charming affair. He was really everyone's pet, and there was a happy little flurry whenever he stopped to talk to a group of guests.

In another moment his heart had skipped a beat. There was the beautiful Miss Fanny, sitting all by herself in a wide window seat, her long skirt spread out around her. She looked at him with her large dark eyes and smiled. He hurried across the room and sat down beside her. No harm in sitting down and talking, surely.

The Cambridge lady who was giving the party watched them out of the corner of her eye. Well, at last! she sighed.

From then on, Henry Longfellow could be seen almost every afternoon walking across the bridge to Boston to call at the Appletons. In just a few weeks, the joyous news was out for their families and friends. Henry and Fanny were engaged! They were to be married in July!

Henry wrote to his mother in Portland, "I write you one line, and only one, to tell you of the good fortune which has just come to me, namely that I am engaged!"

He wrote to his father, to his sisters and brothers, to his friends on both sides of the ocean.

Their wedding at Miss Fanny's home was a most fashionable affair. When Henry and Fanny Longfellow returned from their wedding trip, they moved into the whole Craigie House. Fanny's father had bought it and given it to them for a wedding present.

As Fanny and Henry Longfellow walked through the big, heavy front door with its iron knocker and its key that was seven inches long, Fanny gazed happily at the beautiful staircase. She looked through the door on her left into the parlor and through the door on her right into the room that was to be Henry's study.

"I love this house," said Fanny. "I think it is the most beautiful house in Cambridge."

"We are going to spend many happy years here together," he promised her.

CHAPTER 9
THE HAPPY POET

ENRY'S PROMISE came true. He and Fanny did live in Craigie House for long, peaceful, and happy years. Their circle of friends grew as people learned to know their generous hospitality. Sometimes they gave large parties. Sometimes just a few of their favorite friends came to dinner— Emerson, Hawthorne, Sumner.

Fanny arranged Henry's study for him where he could work and have his favorite books. Its two front windows looked toward the Charles River when the wooden shutters were open. In back of the study was the music room and library where his other books were kept and where Fanny had her writing desk. His old study directly above him became a playroom for Charles, who was born during the first year of their marriage, and for Ernest, who was born during the second year. Sometimes the poet found it difficult to concentrate until Fanny had put Charles and Ernest to bed.

"It seemed somewhat as if the old study has descended through the floor," he wrote in his journal one evening. "Alas! The old study, now given up as a playroom to noisy Charles, whose feet incessantly patter over my head."

Henry's eyes sometimes bothered him if he overstrained them with reading. So, in the evening, Fanny often read aloud to him as they sat by the fireplace in the music room and library.

She read from the classics and from books written by Henry's friends—Ralph Waldo Emerson or Nathaniel Hawthorne. Henry

Longfellow was watching Hawthorne's work with great interest. He believed that Hawthorne would be one of America's great writers someday.

One evening Nathaniel Hawthorne and a friend stopped in to have dinner with the Longfellows. As they sat around the table chatting, Hawthorne said, "Have you heard the story of how the Acadian farmers were banished from their village?"

Henry Longfellow wanted to hear the story, and Hawthorne and his friend related it for him.

"It's an appealing story," said the friend. "I've been trying to persuade Hawthorne to write a novel about it."

"I don't think it is suitable for a novel," said Hawthorne.

Henry Longfellow was keenly interested. "Are you sure you don't want to write a novel about it?" he asked Hawthorne.

"Quite sure," said Hawthorne. "It doesn't appeal to me."

"Well then," said Longfellow, "let me have the idea for a poem."

"All right," laughed Hawthorne. "I'm sure you will make it into a beautiful poem."

Henry Longfellow thought a great deal about the Acadian story, and he read about the history of the Acadian farmers before he started to work on it. "Evangeline" would be the heroine's name, he decided. At last his pencil began to move over the paper:

This is the forest primeval . . .

He worked all through the winter in every spare moment. From time to time Hawthorne wrote to him from Salem, "How is the poem coming along?"

On the 27th of February, 1847, the long poem was finished. Many of Longfellow's friends had advised him not to write it. A long poem couldn't be a success, they warned. Longfellow ignored their warnings.

"The manuscript has gone off to the printer," he told all of his friends happily.

Just a few days later, on the seventh of April, he had another piece of joyous news for his friends. A third child, a girl, was born!

"We are going to call her Fanny, for her mother," said the poet.

By summertime, Mrs. Longfellow felt well enough to travel, and she and Henry gathered up their three children—two small boys and the infant Fanny—and went to the seashore in Nahant. When they returned in the autumn, and Professor Longfellow was teaching his classes at Harvard again, his book "Evangeline" was selling everywhere. Thousands of copies!

"Evangeline" was the most beautiful poem Longfellow had written so far. It was praised in papers in America and England. Congratulations came in letters from Hawthorne and Emerson and dozens of others. The students at Harvard were prouder than ever of their professor. The people of Cambridge, Portland, Nahant, and everywhere else that Longfellow had ever been, boasted that he was *their* poet.

The sad and beautiful story of the Acadian maiden, Evangeline, and her sweetheart, Gabriel, grew more famous with each passing day.

CHAPTER 10

"EVANGELINE"

WITH VIVID words Longfellow described the happy French Village in Canada where Evangeline had lived with her father. It was the Acadian land, on the shores of the Basin of Minas, distant, secluded, still, and it was called Grand-Pré.

Although Evangeline was only seventeen, she could spin and cook as well as the other ladies in the town. She wore a white cap over her brown hair, and her eyes were as black as the berry that grew on the thorn by the wayside.

When the story began, many young men in the town were in love with Evangeline, but she was interested in only one: Gabriel, son of Basil the blacksmith. In the autumn, when the harvests were gathered, Evangeline and Gabriel planned to be married. The whole village was joyous about the coming wedding. The Acadians planned a great feast and celebration for the bride and groom.

Under the open sky, in the orchard, they spread the long tables of food. The fiddler played lively tunes, beating time with his wooden shoes, while the couples danced and whirled merrily. Suddenly, in the midst of the fun and dancing, the bell sounded in the tower, and drum beats were heard over the meadows. That meant that all the men must gather in the church house to hear an order. There had been ships riding at anchor in the harbor, ships full of soldiers. No one quite knew why they were there.

The order explained why, and it was tragic news. All of their lands and cattle were forfeited to the Crown, and the Acadians of Grand-Pré were to be transported to other lands, scattered far and wide.

"Prisoners now I declare you; for such is his Majesty's pleasure!" declared the officer in charge.

Basil the blacksmith shouted angrily, "Down with the tyrants of England! We never have sworn them allegiance! Death to these foreign soldiers, who seize our homes and our harvests!"

But Father Felician, the village priest, spoke more gently. Raising his hand, with a gesture he awed them into silence and spoke.

"What is this that ye do, my children? What madness has seized you? Forty years of my life have I labored among you, and taught you, not in word alone, but in deed, to love one another!"

They were calmed by his words, but they wept with sorrow, because they knew they must leave their village forever. They must carry their belongings to the seashore to go aboard the ships, to be taken nobody knew where.

Halfway down to the shore, Evangeline waited in silence. She felt calm until she saw Gabriel looking so pale. Tears filled her eyes, and she ran to meet him.

"Gabriel! Be of good cheer! For if we love one another, nothing, in truth, can harm us, whatever mischances may happen!"

But the whole thing had happened so quickly that people and goods became mixed up. Families were separated. Evangeline thought her heart would break when she saw Gabriel taken out to a different ship without her. In the terrible confusion, even husbands and wives were separated, and children were left behind.

In despair, Evangeline stood on the shore with her father. They were only at the beginning of their troubles, for their cottages were set afire. When Evangeline's father saw the great red flames, he sank down upon the beach and closed his eyes. He had died of grief.

Father Felician took Evangeline aboard one of the ships, and they sailed away. The Acadians landed on separate coasts—scattered like flakes of snow. Friendless, homeless, hopeless, they wandered from city to city, from the cold lakes of the North to the sultry southern savannas.

The maiden Evangeline could not rest anywhere until she found Gabriel. She and Father Felician wandered on, asking wherever they went if anyone had seen Gabriel.

"Oh, yes! We have seen him," they told her in one place. "He was with Basil the blacksmith, and both have gone to the prairies." Another said, "He went South. He is in the lowlands of Louisiana." Often she would be told, "Dear child! Why dream and wait for him longer? Are there not other youths as fair as Gabriel?"

But she would always reply sadly, "I cannot! Whither my heart has gone, there follows my hand, and not elsewhere."

Evangeline never gave up hope. She wandered on and on, searching for Gabriel. Once, when she and Father Felician were traveling down a river in Louisiana, their boat passed close to Gabriel's in the night. Gabriel was traveling to the West, weary with waiting, unhappy and restless. As soon as Evangeline learned that Gabriel had gone West, she traveled after him, far into the land of Indian trails, near the Ozark Mountains. The Indians told her Gabriel had gone farther north, and she went on.

She heard that he had built a lodge by the banks of the Saginaw River, deep in the Michigan forests. But when, after weary days, by long and perilous marches, she reached the place—she found the hunter's lodge deserted and fallen to ruin.

Thus did the years glide on, and the maiden was seen wandering in secluded hamlets, in towns and cities, always searching for Gabriel. She was fair and young when she started

her journey, but she was faded and old when she finished. When her hair was gray and she was no longer beautiful, she came to the city of Philadelphia. There she decided to stay, working as a Sister of Mercy, visiting the sick and the poor.

One Sunday morning she entered the almshouse, where the oldest and poorest and most wretched of folk were kept. Evangeline walked among the rows of beds. Suddenly she stopped. Her face turned deathly white, and she cried out. On the pallet before her was stretched the form of an old man.

> Motionless, senseless, dying, he lay, and his spirit exhausted
> Seemed to be sinking down through infinite depths in the darkness,
> Darkness of slumber and death, forever sinking and sinking.
> Then through those realms of shade, in multiplied reverberations,
> Heard he that cry of pain, and through the hush that succeeded
> Whispered a gentle voice, in accents tender and saint-like,
> "Gabriel! O my beloved!" and died away into silence.

~

> Vainly he strove to rise; and Evangeline, kneeling beside him,
> Kissed his dying lips, and laid his head on her bosom.
> Sweet was the light of his eyes; but it suddenly sank into darkness,
> As when a lamp is blown out by a gust of wind at a casement.
> All was ended now, the hope, and the fear, and the sorrow,

All the aching of heart, the restless, unsatisfied longing,
All the dull, deep pain, and constant anguish of patience!
And, as she pressed once more the lifeless head to
 her bosom,
Meekly she bowed her own, and murmured, "Father, I
 thank thee!"

CHAPTER 11
"THE BUILDING OF THE SHIP"

O NCE, LONG ago, Longfellow's father had advised him that no one could earn a living writing poetry. Others had given him the same advice. They were all wrong. "Evangeline" was selling thousands of copies. It was going to be published in England; and later on, it would be translated into other languages.

The sorrow that Longfellow so often put into his poems soon cast a shadow over his own life. The baby, Fanny, at the end of her second summer, became ill. She lay in bed, still and burning with fever in the August heat.

Fanny and Henry looked at each other terrified. The boys had been sick now and then, but never as sick as this.

"Henry, I'm so frightened!" was all that Mrs. Longfellow would say.

Everything else in the Longfellow household stopped as the doctor came day after day. Even Ernest and Charles, usually so noisy, were quiet, peeking in once in a while to look at their tiny sister. At first, she took a turn for the better, then she grew worse.

"Little Fanny is weak and miserable; which way will the balance of life and death turn?" said Henry Longfellow.

Now and then a moan from the child, but that was all. On the eleventh of September the poet went to his study, closed the door, and sadly wrote in his diary:

"At half-past four this afternoon she died. Her breathing grew fainter, fainter, then ceased without a sigh, without a flutter—perfectly quiet, perfectly painless. The sweetest expression was on her face."

Longfellow never wrote about his most secret feelings, not even in his diary. He kept them to himself always, and nobody could really know how much he suffered in his heart when his daughter died. There was only one poem that gave a hint, and he didn't publish it until two years later. It was called "Resignation." It began:

> There is no flock, however watched and tended,
> But one dead lamb is there!

It ended:

> By silence sanctifying, not concealing,
> The grief that must have way.

When the two boys came down with the mumps later on, Henry and Fanny watched over them constantly. They didn't want to lose any more children.

The poet, whom so many people loved, didn't publish another book of verse until 1850. *The Seaside and the Fireside* was the name of the next volume, and it was a collection of short poems. The seaside in the summer and the fireside at Craigie House in the winter were the two places Longfellow loved best. The poem in the new collection that everyone liked best was "The Building of the Ship."

While he was writing "The Building of the Ship," Longfellow was once more a small boy sitting on the docks of Portland,

watching the ships and the sailors from all over the world,
watching new ships being built.

> Day by day the vessel grew,
> With timbers fashioned strong and true,
> Stemson and keelson and sternson-knee,
> Till, framed with perfect symmetry,
> A skeleton ship rose up to view!
>
> ∼
>
> With oaken brace and copper band,
> Lay the rudder on the sand.
>
> ∼
>
> Behold, at last,
> Each tall and tapering mast
> Is swung into its place;
> Shrouds and stays
> Holding it firm and fast!
>
> ∼
>
> All is finished! and at length
> Has come the bridal day
> Of beauty and of strength.
> Today the vessel shall be launched!
>
> ∼
>
> All around them and below,
> The sound of hammers, blow on blow,
> Knocking away the shores and spurs.
> And see! she stirs!
> She starts—she moves—she seems to feel
> The thrill of life along her keel,
> And, spurning with her foot the ground,
> With one exulting, joyous bound,
> She leaps into the ocean's arms!
>
> ∼

Sail forth into the sea, O ship!
Through wind and wave, right onward steer!

Thou, too, sail on, O Ship of State!
Sail on, O Union, strong and great!
Humanity with all its fears,
With all the hopes of future years,
Is hanging breathless on thy fate!

Henry Longfellow was a truly American poet writing about America. Once, many years before, he had said there ought to be important American writers. He had hoped to be one of them, and his dream was coming true.

He was already thinking about another American subject for a long poem: the Indians. He couldn't quite decide, though, just what meter he wanted to use. There was no hurry. He continued to think about it while his home life and his teaching went on.

It was a happy day for him when he took his own two boys to their first day at school. Down the streets of Cambridge he went, holding Charles by one hand and Ernest by the other. It reminded him of his own first day at school. Fanny was waiting for him when he returned to the house.

"I left them sitting in their little chairs among the other children," he reported to her with a big smile. "God bless the little fellows!"

There was still more happiness in store for Henry and Fanny Longfellow when another girl was born.

"She will take the place of the little one we lost," sighed Fanny.

Alice was the new child's name; Alice had dark hair, and her blue eyes were a contrast to her brother Ernest's black ones.

When Alice was three years old, and Charles and Ernest were nine and eight, the Longfellows had another daughter with golden hair, Edith.

"Now I have four children," boasted Henry Longfellow. "Two boys and two girls."

His novels and poetry were becoming so successful, and selling so many thousands of copies, that by the time Henry Longfellow was forty-seven years old, he was able to retire from teaching at Harvard and devote himself to writing.

He was up early every morning, sometimes at six. He worked for an hour or two, then went for a walk—often taking the two boys to school. Then back to his study for work. Winter afternoons found him out on the front lawn helping his children build snow palaces. He took them to the museum or to the circus or to the library at Harvard to look at the big books of Audubon's birds.

Summers usually found the whole Longfellow family at the seashore at Nahant.

George Washington Greene had returned from Italy and was teaching languages at Brown University in nearby Rhode Island. He and Longfellow could visit and chat about their travels in Europe. Longfellow was glad to learn that Greene was writing a biography about his famous grandfather, General Nathanael Greene.

By this time Longfellow had his idea for a long poem about the Indians well in mind and was working hard on it.

"I think I've got it at last," he had told Fanny one day, and she knew just what he meant.

"You mean your Indian poem, don't you?"

"Yes. I know at last how I want to write it. I shall use the style and meter of a Scandinavian poem I once read."

The Indian maidens and warriors that he had imagined when he was a small boy were coming to life on paper. Carefully he worked on his poem day after day, writing in pencil and copying

it over in ink for the printer. He sat at a round table with a green cloth cover. And he had a wooden platform on the table in front of him on which he worked.

His Indian hero's name was "Hiawatha," and Longfellow searched into the old records about the Indians who had lived in the Great Lakes country.

CHAPTER 12

"Hiawatha"

HIAWATHA WAS the hero and strong protector of the Ojibway people. His father was the West Wind. His mother, Wenonah, had died of sorrow; and his grandmother, Nokomis, took care of him when he was a child.

> By the shores of Gitche Gumee,
> By the shining Big-Sea-Water,
> Stood the wigwam of Nokomis,
> Daughter of the Moon, Nokomis,
> Dark behind it rose the forest,
> Rose the black and gloomy pine-trees,
> Rose the firs with cones upon them;
> Bright before it beat the water,
> Beat the clear and sunny water,
> Beat the shining Big-Sea-Water.

At the door of the wigwam on summer evenings, Hiawatha sat and listened to the whispering pine trees, the lapping water, and the sounds of the forest. During the days, with his grandmother's help, he learned the secrets of nature.

> Then the little Hiawatha
> Learned of every bird its language,
> Learned their names and all their secrets,

How they built their nests in Summer,
Where they hid themselves in Winter,
Talked with them whene'er he met them,
Called them "Hiawatha Chickens."

He called the wild animals of the forest "Hiawatha's Brothers."
The beaver, the squirrel, the reindeer, and the rabbit, all became
his friends.

Hiawatha learned to hunt with a bow and arrow. He grew
strong and swift of foot, and he was brave. When he became a
young man, he fought many times with the enemies of his people
and defeated them.

One problem of the Ojibway people worried Hiawatha—
they needed a new kind of food. They had the blueberry, the
strawberry, the fish, and the wild animals; but these were not
enough. As Hiawatha walked through the forest, he met the
young god Mondamin.

And behold! the young Mondamin,
With his soft and shining tresses,
With his garments green and yellow,
With his long and glossy plumage . . .

Hiawatha and Mondamin fought; they wrestled for seven
days. At last Hiawatha was triumphant.

Suddenly upon the greensward
All alone stood Hiawatha,
Panting with his wild exertion,
Palpitating with the struggle;
And before him breathless, lifeless,
Lay the youth, with hair dishevelled,
Plumage torn, and garments tattered,
Dead he lay there in the sunset.

Hiawatha's Sailing.
~~The Birch Canoe~~:

"Give me of thy bark, O Birch Tree,
Of thy yellow bark, O Birch Tree,
Growing by the ~~rushing~~ ~~river~~
Tall and stately in the valley,
I a light canoe will build me,
Build a swift chee-maun for sailing,
That shall float upon the river
~~Like the yellow~~ leaf in Autumn, —
~~As a yellow water-lily.~~"
Thus aloud cried Hiawatha
In the solitary forest,
When the birds were singing gayly,
When the buds and leaves were shooting,
And the sun from sleep awaking,
Started up and said "Here am I:"
With his knife the tree he girdled,
Underneath its lowest branches,
Just above the roots he cut it,

From original manuscript of "Hiawatha"

Hiawatha buried Mondamin and watched over his grave. At last a small green feather, like the ones Mondamin had worn, began to sprout up from the grave. Then another and another grew. By the end of the summer there stood the corn in all its beauty—the new food for the Ojibways and Hiawatha's great gift to his people!

Hiawatha went on to new adventures. He built a birch-bark canoe:

"Give me of your bark, O Birch-tree!
Of your yellow bark, O Birch-tree!
Growing by the rushing river,
Tall and stately in the valley!
I a light canoe will build me,
Build a swift Cheemaun for sailing,
That shall float upon the river,
Like a yellow leaf in Autumn,
Like a yellow water-lily!"

Hiawatha's bride was Minnehaha, and he talked over his wedding plans with his grandmother, Nokomis:

"In the land of the Dacotahs
Lives the Arrow-maker's daughter,
Minnehaha, Laughing Water,
Handsomest of all the women.
I will bring her to your wigwam,
She shall run upon your errands,
Be your starlight, moonlight, firelight,
Be the sunlight of my people!"

For many years Hiawatha and his wife Minnehaha looked after the Ojibway Indians. Those were happy, peaceful years. The Ojibways grew corn, hunted in the forests, built birch-bark canoes, made sugar from the maple, gathered wild rice from the meadows, and dressed the skins of deer and beaver for clothing. Until at last, when Hiawatha was old, and he knew he must leave the Ojibways, he climbed into his birch-bark canoe for the last time.

> Westward, westward Hiawatha
> Sailed into the fiery sunset,
> Sailed into the purple vapors,
> Sailed into the dusk of evening.
>   And the people from the margin
> Watched him floating, rising, sinking,
> Till the birch canoe seemed lifted
> High into that sea of splendor,
> Till it sank into the vapors
> Like the new moon slowly, slowly
> Sinking in the purple distance.
>   And they said, "Farewell forever!"
> Said, "Farewell, O Hiawatha!"
> And the forests, dark and lonely,
> Moved through all their depths of darkness,
> Sighed, "Farewell, O Hiawatha!"

CHAPTER 13

WAR AND SORROW

H ENRY LONGFELLOW's family gathered around him as he read letters and newspaper articles about "Hiawatha." Alice and Edith clambered over the arms of his chair, while eleven-year-old Charles and ten-year-old Ernest sat cross-legged on the floor. Fanny sat by the fireplace with the new baby, Allegra, in her arms.

Messages of praise came in from near and far. Never had a poem been so successful. The idea of the Indian hero, Hiawatha, became so popular that sculptors made statues of the Ojibway chieftain, and artists painted pictures of him and Minnehaha. The book was translated into other languages, and people all over the world became interested in the American Indians.

"I must write a poem about another American subject," said Longfellow.

He didn't have to think very long about it. What other important American subject was there? Why, the Pilgrims, of course! Some of his own ancestors had been Pilgrims. When Longfellow looked back into the family records, he found one named John Alden. John Alden had been with the little company of Puritans who came to America seeking religious freedom. They had come in the *Mayflower* that landed on the shores of Massachusetts in 1620, and they had founded the colony of Plymouth. John Alden had married Priscilla Mullins, and Henry Longfellow's mother had descended directly from them. The love story of John Alden and Priscilla grew in Henry Longfellow's imagination while he sat in his study and thought about it.

He decided to tell the story of how they met and fell in love and married. He would tell the story of how Captain Miles Standish wanted to marry Priscilla, too, and sent John Alden to speak for him. Priscilla sat at her spinning wheel, listening to John Alden tell her how brave and good Captain Miles Standish was.

> Archly the maiden smiled and, with eyes
> overrunning with laughter,
> Said, in a tremulous voice, "Why don't
> you speak for yourself, John?"

Henry Longfellow finished writing "The Courtship of Miles Standish" three years after his "Hiawatha." "Miles Standish" was full of the life of the Plymouth colony. It told the customs of the Pilgrims, of their homes, their bravery, their wars with the Indians.

"Miles Standish" was another triumph for Longfellow. No other poet anywhere was as popular and as loved as he. He sat in his beautiful and peaceful Craigie House in Cambridge, reading great stacks of mail from admirers.

But the rest of the United States was not as peaceful and happy as the village of Cambridge. Henry Longfellow couldn't spend all of his time studying and writing about days gone by.

Troubled times were brewing. War clouds were gathering, and Longfellow's two sons were growing to manhood. Charles was seventeen, old enough to be a soldier.

Both Henry and Fanny Longfellow were opposed to wars and fighting. Sometimes in the evenings when Emerson visited them, they sat talking about slavery and other problems that were creating so much trouble.

Charles Sumner was a United States senator by then, making stirring speeches in Washington for the abolition of slavery.

Abraham Lincoln was elected president in 1860, and Longfellow was happy and hopeful about it.

"This is a great victory," he said. "It is the redemption of the country. Freedom is triumphant."

When he and Emerson and others in the North heard that South Carolina was going to secede from the United States, they knew the situation was grave. Other states were leaving the United States. There was war talk everywhere. If Longfellow went to Boston to hear a speaker, the speaker talked of war. If he went to church, the sermon was about war. If he read the papers, the news was about war.

"Ghastly!" was all he could say. "How can we have peace if people never think of peace?"

These were the times when he loved his home best, loved the quiet and peace of his study, loved that hour between the dark and daylight, when his workday was finished and his three little girls could invade his study. It was the hour he called "The Children's Hour":

> Between the dark and daylight,
> When the night is beginning to lower,
> Comes a pause in the day's occupations,
> That is known as the Children's Hour.
> I hear in the chamber above me
> The patter of little feet,
> The sound of a door that is opened,
> And voices soft and sweet.
> From my study I see in the lamplight,
> Descending the broad hall stair,
> Grave Alice, and laughing Allegra,

And Edith with golden hair.
A whisper, and then a silence:
Yet I know by their merry eyes
They are plotting and planning together
To take me by surprise.
A sudden rush from the stairway,
A sudden raid from the hall!
By three doors left unguarded
They enter my castle wall!
They climb up into my turret
O'er the arms and back of my chair;
If I try to escape, they surround me;
They seem to be everywhere.
They almost devour me with kisses,
Their arms about me entwine,
Till I think of the Bishop of Bingen
In his Mouse-Tower on the Rhine!
Do you think, O blue-eyed banditti,
Because you have scaled the wall,
Such an old mustache as I am
Is not a match for you all!
I have you fast in my fortress,
And will not let you depart,
But put you down into the dungeon
In the round-tower of my heart.
And there will I keep you forever,
Yes, forever and a day,
Till the walls shall crumble to ruin,
And moulder in dust away!

But Longfellow wasn't safe from tragedy, even in his home.

As he sat in his study one day, Fanny sat in the library at her writing desk. Edith and Allegra were with her. Longfellow could hear their laughter from time to time because Fanny was clipping off pieces of the girls' curls to send to their aunts and uncles. As she popped each curl into an envelope with its letter, she held a lighted candle to the end of a stick of wax. A drop of wax would fall on the back of the envelope and seal it shut.

It was a hot July day, and Mrs. Longfellow was wearing a fluffy, light muslin dress. While Edith and Allegra stood at each side of her chair, clapping their hands as a curl was ready to go into the mail, the candle flame licked a corner of Mrs. Longfellow's sleeve.

Her clothing caught fire in an instant, and the flames shot up toward her face.

She jumped up from the chair and screamed as a breeze from the French window made the fire spread over her whole dress. Henry Longfellow heard the screams and opened the door between his study and the library. In panic, covered in flames, Fanny ran toward him. He grabbed a rug and wrapped it around her as she moaned and fainted.

Fanny Longfellow never regained consciousness. When the doctor came rushing into the house and saw her terrible burns, he shook his head. By the next morning, she was dead.

Henry Longfellow was beside himself with grief. He couldn't rest. He couldn't think. He couldn't talk to anyone.

"Your own hands and face are badly burned," said the doctor, but Longfellow paid him no heed.

The burns on his face were so bad that even after they healed he was unable to shave. That was why he allowed his beard to grow.

After eighteen years of happiness with Fanny Appleton, Henry Longfellow was crushed, heartbroken, lost. Although he was only fifty-four, he felt like an aging man. His hair became much grayer than it had been.

He returned to his writing, to his walks, and his talks with Emerson and Hawthorne. Sometimes he got into the carriage and went for a drive. Even though he had three daughters to look after him, he would be a lonely man for the rest of his life.

Friends and admirers came from all over the world to visit the great poet Longfellow. They came from Italy, from Spain, from France, from Scandinavia, from Germany and England. Many spoke no English, but that didn't matter because Longfellow could speak so many languages. The housekeeper at Craigie House was always opening the door to visitors and showing them into the poet's study.

Charles was home that tragic summer and through the winter, but the next spring his father had to bid him goodbye. Charles Longfellow had joined the Massachusetts Cavalry, and he had to go to war with his outfit.

On a dreary, rainy March day, Henry Longfellow and Charles climbed into a carriage and drove over muddy roads to town. There Charles was to go aboard the ship that would take him southward.

They talked little on the way. Charles knew how hard it was for his father to give up another member of the family.

"I'll be back soon," he promised. "The Civil War won't last very long."

"Wars always last longer than you expect them to," said Longfellow.

After Charles left, the poet seemed quieter and dreamier than before. He didn't argue about war. He didn't make any stirring speeches about abolishing slavery, the way many of his friends did. He just kept his griefs to himself.

Summer at Nahant was dull, the town deserted with so many away. Through autumn and winter, the war dragged on. At Christmastime, Ernest and the three girls decorated a Christmas tree, and the poet tried to be merry for their sakes. But they all understood that he was worried about Charles. They were worried about Charles, too, because he was in the midst of battle.

Letters and messages from the front came in once in a while. One time they heard that Charles was sick with camp fever. In March he was made a second lieutenant. By May they heard he was in camp somewhere on the Potomac River.

Another Christmas was almost at hand when the Longfellows heard the news they dreaded most. Charles had been badly wounded, said a telegram from Washington.

Henry Longfellow dropped everything he was doing and journeyed down to Washington. Ernest went with him.

Of course, America's most popular poet was recognized as he hurried around Washington trying to find out when the trainload of wounded soldiers would arrive.

A great, lusty man in a uniform and high boots stopped him in the railroad station and asked, "Are you Professor Longfellow? Well, I am from Riga, and I have just translated your 'Hiawatha' into Russian."

At that moment Longfellow was more interested in Charles than in "Hiawatha," but he chatted politely with the man until the train came in.

Charles had been shot through both shoulders, and the doctor said his wounds would need a lot of care and take a long time to heal. His father and brother took him carefully home to Cambridge, where they put him to bed, and the family doctor looked after him.

CHAPTER 14
THE FRIEND OF CHILDREN

A
FTER THE war the poet's life became peaceful again. He was able to spend his winters at Craigie House and his summers at Nahant.

Charles recovered from his wounds. He loved the sea as much as his father did, and he became a famous yachtsman, sailing all over the world. Along with other gifts, he once brought his father a gift of fine tea all the way from China.

Ernest became an artist and started his own school of painting. When he married, he moved into a house across the street from Craigie House.

The three girls lived at home, looking after their father, while they grew to be young ladies. Edith was the first to marry, but not until after her father was seventy-one. Then he saw his "Edith with golden hair" wedded to Richard Dana.

As the years passed, Henry Longfellow's hair and beard became snow white, and the small children around Cambridge couldn't remember that he had ever looked any other way.

Children loved Henry Longfellow as much as they loved his poetry. They invaded his study whenever his daughters would let them. Often a young visitor would come away with a piece of verse written just for him.

Even when the poet was past seventy, he went out sturdily for his walks and visited Nahant in the summer. Or sometimes his

neighbors would see him driving by in an open victoria drawn by two high-stepping black horses.

When he reached seventy-two, the children of Cambridge gathered together their pennies and dimes and gave their favorite poet an armchair for his birthday. The chair was made from the very chestnut tree that had stood by the blacksmith's shop in Cambridge, the one about which Longfellow had written "The Village Blacksmith."

Of course, he answered the children of Cambridge with a poem, "From My Armchair":

> Am I a king, that I should call my own
> This splendid ebon throne?
> Or by what reason, or what right divine,
> Can I proclaim it mine?
> Only, perhaps, by right divine of song
> It may to me belong;
> Only because the spreading chestnut tree
> Of old was sung by me.

After that, whenever a child visited the poet in his study, he was allowed to sit in the armchair, and Longfellow presented him with a copy of the poem.

Henry Longfellow looked so sturdy; he held himself so straight when he went for a stroll; and he carried his walking stick so jauntily, that it seemed as though he would live to be a hundred. After all, his parents had lived to be very old. His father had lived to be seventy-three and Grandfather Wadsworth to be eighty-one.

On a chilly March day, though, when he was seventy-five, Longfellow insisted on taking a walk on the east porch of Craigie House.

"It's too cold a day for you to go out, Father," said Alice.

"Nonsense! I need some air."

"Then please wear your fur-lined coat," pleaded Allegra.

He allowed them to help him into his coat and button it up around his neck. Then out he went to walk up and down the long porch.

The dampness and cold of the early spring day penetrated even through his coat, and later that evening he admitted, "I feel quite ill."

Alice and Allegra hurriedly put him to bed and sent for the doctor. Longfellow lay very still, not saying a word, his strength failing a little each day. He opened his eyes once and saw his sister Anne standing beside his bed. She had traveled up from Portland.

"Now I know that I must be very ill, since you have been sent for," he said in a voice that was no more than a whisper.

All of Cambridge, Portland, Nahant, and Boston, from the youngest to the oldest, waited anxiously for news of their poet. Each day they were told that he was a little weaker. Until, on the sixth day, he passed away.

No American poet has ever been loved by more people than Henry Longfellow, and, although he is gone, his poetry will live forever.

> Such songs have power to quiet
> The restless pulse of care,
> And come like the benediction
> That follows after prayer.
> Then read from the treasured volume
> The poem of thy choice,
> And lend to the rhyme of the poet
> The beauty of thy voice.
> And the night shall be filled with music,
> And the cares, that infest the day,
> Shall fold their tents, like the Arabs,
> And as silently steal away.